# RACIAL JUSTICE IN AMERICA

# What Does It Mean to DEFUND THE POLICE?

## JESSICA S. HENRY WITH KELISA WING

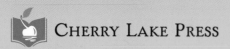

**CHERRY LAKE PRESS**

Published in the United States of America by Cherry Lake Publishing Group
Ann Arbor, Michigan
www.cherrylakepublishing.com

Reading Adviser: Marla Conn, MS, Ed., Literacy specialist, Read-Ability, Inc.
Content Adviser: Kelisa Wing
Book Design and Cover Art: Felicia Macheske

Photo Credits: Library of Congress, Sketch by F.B. Schell/LOC Control No.: 2009630225, 7; © Kerry Lane/Shutterstock.com, 9; © Julian Leshay/Shutterstock.com, 11; © Pix_Arena/Shutterstock.com, 15; © Tippman98x/Shutterstock.com, 17; © SpeedKingz/Shutterstock.com, 18; © Rawpixel.com/Shutterstock.com, 21; © Polarpx/Shutterstock.com, 23; © Anna Kristiana Dave/Shutterstock.com, 27; Library of Congress, Photograph by Bernard Gotfryd,/LOC Control No.: 2006679789, 29; © Victor Moussa/Shutterstock.com, 31

Graphics Throughout: © debra hughes/Shutterstock.com; © GoodStudio/Shutterstock.com; © Natewimon Nantiwat/Shutterstock.com; © Galyna_P/Shutterstock.com

Library of Congress Cataloging-in-Publication Data

Names: Henry, Jessica S., 1969- author. | Wing, Kelisa, author.
Title: What does it mean to defund the police? / Jessica S. Henry, Kelisa Wing.
Description: Ann Arbor, Michigan : Cherry Lake Publishing, [2021] | Series:
   Racial justice in America | Includes bibliographical references and index.
   | Audience: Grades 4-6 | Summary: "Race in America has been avoided in children's
   education for too long. What Does It Mean to Defund the Police? explores the concept
   of defunding while addressing the reasons people are calling for it in a comprehensive,
   honest, and age-appropriate way. Developed in conjunction with educator, advocate,
   and author Kelisa Wing to reach children of all races and encourage them to approach
   race issues with open eyes and minds. Includes 21st Century Skills and content, as well
   as a PBL activity across the Racial Justice in America series. Also includes a table of
   contents, glossary, index, author biography, sidebars, educational matter, and
   activities"— Provided by publisher.
Identifiers: LCCN 2020040017 (print) | LCCN 2020040018 (ebook)
   | ISBN 9781534180260 (hardcover) | ISBN 9781534181977 (paperback)
   | ISBN 9781534181274 (pdf) | ISBN 9781534182981 (ebook)
Subjects: LCSH: Police—United States—Juvenile literature. | Police
   administration—United States—Finance—Juvenile literature. |
   Police-community relations—United States—Juvenile literature. |
   Discrimination in law enforcement—United States—Juvenile literature.
Classification: LCC HV8139 .H46 2021  (print) | LCC HV8139  (ebook) | DDC
   363.2068/1—dc23
LC record available at https://lccn.loc.gov/2020040017
LC ebook record available at https://lccn.loc.gov/2020040018

Cherry Lake Publishing Group would like to acknowledge the work of the Partnership for 21st Century Learning, a Network of Battelle for Kids. Please visit *http://www.battelleforkids.org/networks/p21* for more information.

Printed in the United States of America
Corporate Graphics

**Jessica S. Henry** is a college professor, author, and lawyer who used to be a public defender. She believes that together we can make the world a safer and more just place for all people. You can learn more about her work at jessicahenryjustice.com.

**Kelisa Wing** honorably served in the U.S. Army and has been an educator for 14 years. She is the author of *Promises and Possibilities: Dismantling the School to Prison Pipeline, If I Could: Lessons for Navigating an Unjust World*, and *Weeds & Seeds: How to Stay Positive in the Midst of Life's Storms*. She speaks both nationally and internationally about discipline reform, equity, and student engagement. Kelisa lives in Northern Virginia with her husband and two children.

# CHAPTER 1

# Calls for Change in Policing

In the spring and summer of 2020, people filled the streets to peacefully protest. They expressed their outrage and frustration about the unequal treatment by the police of people of color. People marched, chanted, and made signs that expressed their beliefs. They demanded an end to racism in police practices and firmly stated that "Black lives matter." Some protesters called for governments to defund or abolish the police.

What sparked those protests?

George Floyd was a Black man who was killed by police officers in Minneapolis, Minnesota, on May 25, 2020. His death was recorded on a cell phone camera, and the video was viewed by millions of people around the world.

People were horrified by what they saw on the video. They believed that the officers who killed George Floyd acted in a way that was unfair and unjust. People were especially angry because it was not the first time something like this had happened. Breonna Taylor, Michael Brown, Stephon Clark, Alton Sterling, and Atatiana Jefferson are just some of Black and brown people killed by the police in recent years.

People called for the police to stop using deadly force against people of color. They also wanted the police to stop the aggressive policing tactics that unfairly impacted people of color and those living in underserved communities.

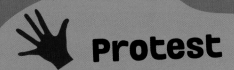 **Protest**

One way to make your voice heard is to join with others in peaceful protest. You can make signs, chant words, sing songs, and walk side by side with friends, family, and other people to stand up for what you believe.

# CHAPTER 2

# Policing Yesterday and Today

One of the earliest forms of American policing were slave patrols in the American South, which were first formed in 1704 in South Carolina. These slave patrols were tasked with watching, catching, and even beating enslaved people. The primary goals of slave patrols were to enforce laws relating to slavery and prevent revolts by enslaved people.

Slave patrols formally ended when slavery was abolished at the end of the Civil War. But police continued to enforce laws, such as the short-lived Black codes and later Jim Crow laws. These laws limited Black people's freedoms, denied them basic civil rights, and kept them separated from White people.

In the early 1900s, police were often violent and corrupt. Today's police forces are much more organized and professional than they were at the beginning.

But some people argue that the racist history of early law enforcement continues to be felt today.

Officials examining the passes Black people needed to travel in the South in the 1800s.

A police officer's job is to enforce laws, investigate and solve crimes, and keep the public safe. In recent years, their job has grown. They respond to many different kinds of problems, including calls about people with mental health issues, addiction, or family problems. They sometimes work in schools, as well as on the streets in their communities.

Police officers are public servants, which means they are employed by the governments of towns, cities, counties, states, and even countries.

You may have friends and family members who are police officers. People who join the police want to help their communities and often do so at great risk to their personal safety.

How do you describe the police in your community? Do you believe all people experience the police in the same way? Why or why not?

Before people become police officers, they receive training that is supposed to help prepare them for the job. This is important because the police have special rights. Unlike most other jobs, police can carry weapons. Under existing laws, the police can also use force to defend themselves.

But the police cannot use force whenever they want. The force they use must be equal to the threat they believe they face.

Some police officers agree that policing should be reformed.

# CHAPTER 3

# What Does "Defund the Police" Mean?

Governments collect taxes from people in the community. The money that is raised from taxes is used to fund the police. It is also used to fund services in the community.

Some communities devote a large part of their budget to policing. For example, in 2020, New York City spent more on policing than on four agencies (combined) that address health, homeless services, housing, and youth and community development. When people say they want to "defund the police," they mean that governments should reduce the amount of money they spend in their budget on policing. Instead, they want governments to use that money to invest in programs that help the community.

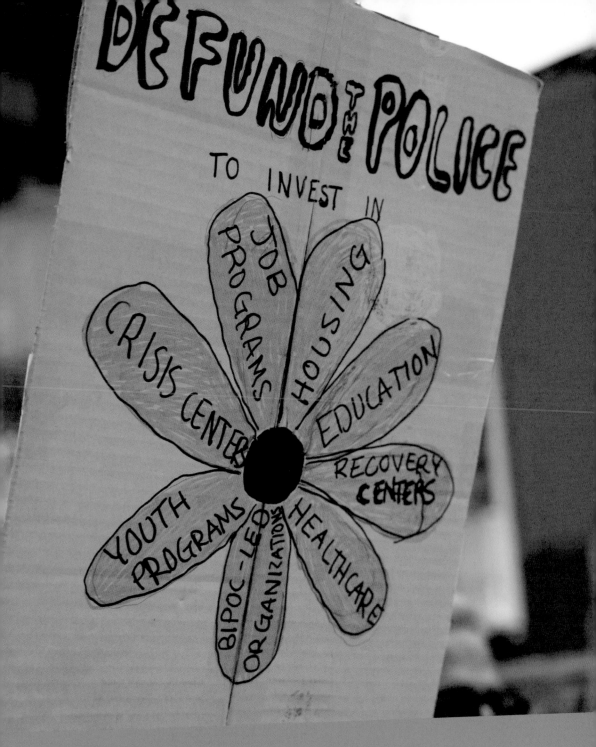

People who want to defund the police believe that investing in social programs will be better for police forces and the communities they serve.

# Funding Activity

Police departments are funded by the type of government that employs them. Local police departments are funded by the city or larger county in which they work. State police departments are funded by the state government. Federal police— like the Federal Bureau of Investigation (FBI)—are funded by the federal government.

Do you want to know how much of your city's budget is spent on policing? Contact the city or town council where you live and ask. Identify additional programs that you would like to see better funded. Write a letter to your city or town council and share your ideas with them.

These programs include social services, housing, education, youth development, jobs training, health care, and other community programs. People who support this view believe that community investment would reduce crime in the long run and increase public safety.

Reformers would also like to see more money invested in specially trained teams of social workers and other crisis managers. Instead of the police, these teams could be the first to respond to certain types of emergencies, such as mental health crises, drug overdoses, family conflicts, or issues involving people who are homeless.

With other community organizations working on those emergencies, the police would be free to focus on more serious crimes. And they would be able to do so with a smaller budget.

# CHAPTER 4

# What Does "Disband the Police" Mean?

Some people want to see their police department disbanded. This means that the department would be shut down, and something else would be created to address public safety.

Shortly after George Floyd was killed, the Minneapolis City Council voted to dissolve the city police department. What they will put in its place is not yet clear. But the city council president said she wanted to create a "new model of public safety that actually keeps our community safe."

George Floyd's murder was a turning point that caused communities to call for changes in policing.

This would not be the first time a police department was disbanded. Camden, New Jersey, had high rates of violent crime and a corrupt police force. In 2012, the city's police department was disbanded because officials decided the existing force could not be repaired. The Camden County Police Department took over law enforcement responsibility.

The new Camden police force created new policing policies. They required newly hired officers to go to the homes of the people who live where the police work. Officers had to introduce themselves and ask about any concerns that residents had. This is not something that the police often do!

Do you know the police in your neighborhood? If an officer asked you what issues you thought should be improved in your neighborhood, what would you say?

The way Camden approached a new way of policing gives other cities a model of what could work for them.

The first role of a police officer is to protect and serve the members of the communities where they work.

Since 2013, violent crime in Camden has dropped 42 percent. Community-oriented policing has improved the relationship between the people who live in Camden and the police who work there. While there is still much work to be done to improve its policing, Camden is an example of a police department that was disbanded and then started again with a new vision of policing.

DO THE WORK!

ESSENTIAL QUESTION

# How can we be anti-racist?

Becoming anti-racist requires actively working against racism using words and actions. This project-based learning assignment will allow you to practice these skills. Read all the books in the *Racial Justice in America* series. Through each "DO THE WORK!" activity, you will research and put together parts of a larger project that will allow you to grow and help others grow as well.

It takes more than punishment to get someone in trouble back on the right track. It takes a group of people who can help. For this portion of your project, you are going to interview your school counselor. As someone who has a background in well-being, mental health, and guiding students, the counselor has an important job. If a student is getting into trouble, what help or resources would the counselor provide to them? Why is it important for a student in trouble to get assistance after coming back to school? After your interview, compare your counselor's responses to the calls for action from reformists who want to defund the police. If some funds were taken from the police and reinvested in the community, what do you think would happen? Are there similarities? Differences? How does this change your understanding of what "defunding the police" means?

For the presentation of your final work, you can create a collage, magazine, podcast, jigsaw puzzle, poem, video, or social media campaign—anything to demonstrate your learning. No matter what you do, just be creative, learn something new, and publicize your work!

# CHAPTER 5

# What Does "Reform the Police" Mean?

Some leaders and activists want to reform the way the police do their jobs. They want to see new rules put in place that make the police more accountable and more effective. They want to change the way that the police enforce the laws in poor communities and communities of color.

But they do not believe that the police should be defunded. In fact, many of the reforms they want would *increase* funding for the police.

In some countries, like Iceland, police officers don't generally carry firearms.

Here are just a few of the ideas that have been suggested:

1.  Reformers have called for improved police training. The police could be trained to de-escalate situations and use nonviolent techniques. This would reduce the potential for harm when they respond to calls. The police also could receive improved racial bias training. This would help increase awareness and reduce the prejudices that they may bring to their jobs and to the interactions they have with the people they serve.

2.  Reformers have called for the increased use of police body cameras and clearer rules about when and how the cameras should be used. Body cameras record the police as they do their job. Cameras create a record of what happens when they interact with people in the communities.

3.  Reformers also want to see officers held responsible when they engage in wrongdoing.

At the heart of the police reform agenda is the idea that current police practices need to be looked at and improved. Reformers believe that with better and different training and policies, police can do their jobs in a way that protects all communities.

Research one of the reform ideas listed on these pages or find one of your own. Share what you learn with your classmates. Based on your research, do you believe any of these ideas could work to reform the police?

# CHAPTER 6

# What Does "Abolish the Police" Mean?

When people say they want to abolish the police, it means that they would like to see a complete end to policing. Called abolitionists, these people argue that we need to create a society where the police are unnecessary. Programs that would prevent the conditions that cause crime in the first place should be created and funded.

Abolitionists want funding to go toward many of the same programs as those who support defunding the police. These programs would create better jobs and job training, affordable housing, quality education, and access to health care that includes treatment for mental health issues and drug addiction. Under this vision, community organizations, rather than the police, would respond to emergency calls.

Some of the Black Lives Matter protesters in the summer of 2020 believe in abolishing the police.

# Angela Davis

Angela Yvonne Davis is a scholar, political activist, and author of numerous books. In the late 1990s, Davis cofounded an organization called Critical Resistance. She called for the abolition of prisons, particularly the systems that make prisons profitable.

Davis herself once spent 16 months in jail while awaiting her day in court for murder charges. She was found not guilty after a criminal trial, but her experience shaped her belief that there should be an end to prisons. Instead, Davis called for investments in education and in building "engaged communities" to address social problems that are too often handled by policing and prisons.

Davis influenced modern activists, such as Mariame Kaba, who call for abolishing the police.

The main difference between those who argue for reducing police budgets and those who call for abolition is the final result. Abolitionists want an end to policing in all circumstances.

Police abolitionists admit that their goal will not be achieved in the immediate future. But they would like to begin the process of creating a "police-free" future by increasing investments in communities.

Angela Davis graduated Brandeis University with honors. She obtained her master's degree from the University of California, San Diego and went on to earn a doctorate in philosophy from Humboldt University in East Berlin.

# CHAPTER 7

# Who Decides?

Whether you believe that police should be defunded, disbanded, abolished, or reformed, the final decision about police funding rests in the hands of our elected government leaders. These leaders vote on a budget. They take the total amount of taxpayer dollars collected and then decide how to spend it. The budget can be thought of as a statement about spending priorities. A budget tells us what our elected leaders believe are the most important issues in their communities—from schools and social programs to law enforcement and prisons.

Local and state elections decide who will set the budget for your town or city. The people who are elected to office determine whether and what reforms are made to police funding. That's why it is very important to vote in all elections.

Voters can choose leaders with similar beliefs about what should be done about the issue of police funding. Voting is a powerful way to make your voice heard and to help make your vision of policing a reality.

# voting

Who we elect as our leaders determines our future. Even if you are not old enough to vote, you can still help. Encourage people to register to vote and to go to the polls on Election Day. Remind them that they need to vote not only in presidential elections but also in local elections. That's because local officials set the budget and decide how to fund a whole range of important programs.

## EXTEND YOUR LEARNING

Elliot, Zetta. *Say Her Name*. Los Angeles, CA: Disney/Jump at the Sun, 2020.

Reynolds, Jason, and Brendan Kiely. *All American Boys*. New York, NY: Atheneum Books, 2017.

Stevenson, Bryan. *Just Mercy: Adapted for Young Adults: A True Story of the Fight for Justice*. New York, NY: Delacorte Press, 2018.

Stone, Nic. *Dear Martin*. New York, NY: Crown, 2017.

Thomas, Angie. *The Hate U Give*. New York, NY: Balzer & Bray, 2017.

## GLOSSARY

**abolish** (uh-BAH-lish) to end or get rid of

**accountable** (uh-KOUNT-uh-buhl) responsible; having to justify or explain something

**aggressive** (uh-GRES-iv) pushy and always ready to attack

**bias** (BYE-uhs) a personal judgment in favor of or against a thing, person, or group, usually in a way considered to be unfair

**Black codes** (BLAK KOHDZ) laws passed immediately after the Civil War ended that greatly limited the rights of Black people

**corrupt** (kuh-RUHPT) dishonest; displaying behavior that doesn't know right from wrong

**crisis** (KRYE-sis) a time of intense difficulty or danger

**de-escalate** (dee-ES-kuh-late) to lessen in intensity, size, or scope

**defend** (dih-FEND) to protect from harm; to guard

**defund** (dee-FUHND) to take money away from a department

**dissolve** (dih-ZOHLV) to end something

**enforce** (en-FORS) to make people follow or obey

**frustration** (fruh-STRAY-shuhn) a feeling of disappointment or helplessness

**investigate** (in-VES-tih-gate) to examine or look into

**Jim Crow** (JIHM KROH) the deeply unfair treatment of Black people in the United States through laws that kept them separate from Whites

**outrage** (OUT-rayj) a strong feeling of anger caused by a wrong or injustice

**prejudices** (PREJ-uh-dis-iz) unreasonable and unfair opinions of someone based on the person's race, religion, or other characteristic

**racism** (RAY-siz-uhm) unfair treatment of people based on the belief that one race is better than another race

**revolts** (rih-VOHLTS) rebellions against a government or an authority

**slave patrols** (SLAYV puh-TROHLZ) organized groups of White men who enforced unfair rules against Black slaves

**social workers** (SOH-shuhl WUR-kurz) people who work to promote the well-being of others by helping

**tactics** (TAK-tiks) methods used to achieve a goal

## INDEX